A FISH
OF THE
WORLD

Terry Jones

A Fish
of the
World

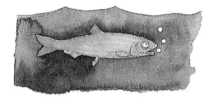

Illustrated by
Michael Foreman

PAVILION

This edition first published in Great Britain in 1993 by
PAVILION BOOKS LIMITED
26 Upper Ground, London SE1 9PD
Text copyright © Terry Jones 1981
Illustrations copyright © Michael Foreman 1981, 1993

This story first appeared in *Fairy Tales* by Terry Jones,
illustrated by Michael Foreman, published in 1981 by
Pavilion Books Limited.

The moral right of the author and illustrator has been asserted.

Designed by Bet Ayer

A CIP catalogue record for this book
is available from the British Library.

ISBN 1 85793 0754

Printed and bound in Singapore by Tien Wah Press Pte Ltd

2 4 6 8 10 9 7 5 3 1

This book may be ordered by post
direct from the publisher. Please contact
the Marketing Department.
But try your bookshop first.

A herring once decided to swim right round the world. 'I'm tired of the North Sea,' he said. 'I want to find out what else there is in the world.'

So he swam off south into the deep Atlantic. He swam and he swam, far far away from the seas he knew, through the warm waters of the Equator and on down into the South Atlantic. And all the time he saw many strange and wonderful fish that he had never seen before. Once he was nearly eaten by a shark, and once he was nearly electrocuted by an electric eel, and once he was nearly stung by a sting-ray.

But he swam on and on, round the tip of Africa
and into the Indian Ocean.
And he passed by devilfish and sailfish and sawfish

and swordfish and bluefish and blackfish and mudfish
and sunfish, and he was amazed by the different shapes
and sizes and colours.

On he swam, into the Java Sea, and he saw fish that
leapt out of the water and fish that lived at the bottom
of the sea and fish that could walk on their fins.

And on he swam, through the Coral Sea, where the
shells of millions and millions of tiny creatures had
turned to rock and stood as big as mountains.

But still he swam on, into the wide Pacific. He swam
over the deepest parts of the ocean, where the water is
so deep that it is inky black at the bottom, and the fish
carry lanterns over their heads, and some have lights
on their tails.

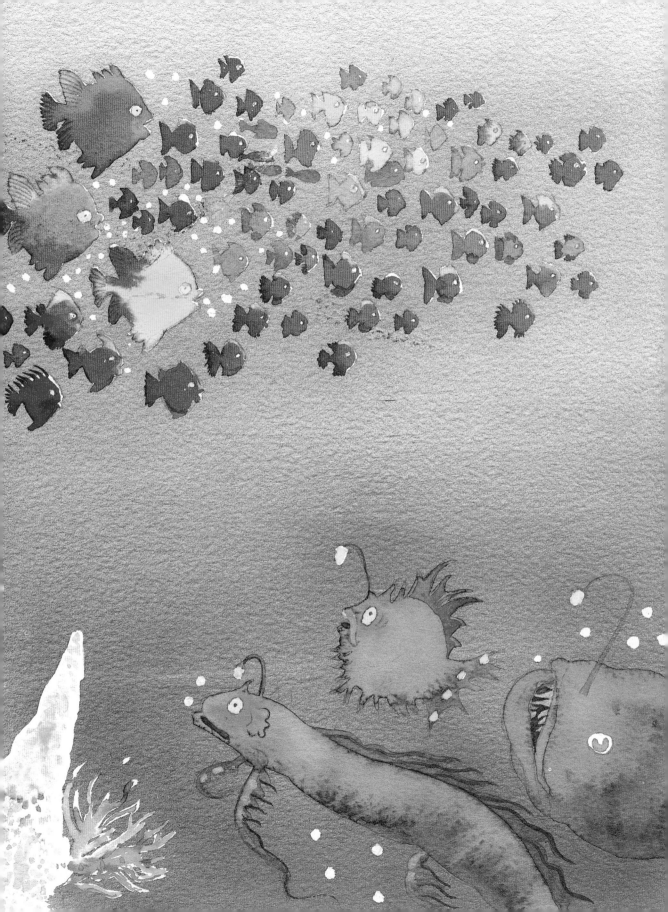

And through the Pacific he swam, and then he
turned north and headed up to the cold Siberian Sea,
where huge white icebergs sailed past him like mighty
ships. And still he swam on and on and into the frozen
Arctic Ocean, where the sea is forever covered in ice.

And on he went, past Greenland and Iceland, and finally he swam home into his own North Sea.

All his friends and relations gathered round and made a great fuss of him. They had a big feast and offered him the very best food they could find.

But the herring just yawned and said: 'I've swum round the entire world. I have seen everything there is to see, and I have eaten more exotic and wonderful dishes than you could possibly imagine.' And he refused to eat anything.

Then his friends and relations begged him to come home and live with them, but he refused. 'I've been everywhere there is, and that old rock is too dull and small for me.' And he went off and lived on his own.

And when the breeding season came, he refused to join in the spawning, saying: 'I've swum round the entire world, and now I know how many fish there are in the world, I can't be interested in herrings any more.'

Eventually, one of the oldest of the herrings swam up to him, and said: 'Listen. If you don't spawn with us, some herrings' eggs will go unfertilized and will not turn into healthy young herring. If you don't live with your family, you'll make them sad. And if you don't eat, you'll die.'

But the herring said: 'I don't mind. I've been everywhere there is to go, I've seen everything there is to see, and now I know everything there is to know.'

The old fish shook his head. 'No one has ever seen everything there is to see,' he said, 'nor known everything there is to know.'

'Look,' said the herring, 'I've swum through the North Sea, the Atlantic Ocean, the Indian Ocean, the Java Sea, the Coral Sea, the great Pacific Ocean, the Siberian Sea and the frozen Arctic. Tell me, what else is there for me to see or know?'

'I don't know,' said the old herring, 'but there may be something.'

Well, just then a fishing boat came by, and the herrings

were caught in a net and taken to market that very day.

And a man bought the herring, and ate it for his supper.

And he never knew that it had swum right round the world, and had seen everything there was to see, and knew everything there was to know.